ABOMIN

®PEARL

MY BEST FRIEND IS A
YETI!

Adapted by Patty Michaels
Illustrated by Patrick Spaziante

Ready-to-Read

Simon Spotlight

New York   London   Toronto   Sydney   New Delhi

SIMON SPOTLIGHT

An imprint of Simon & Schuster Children's Publishing Division

1230 Avenue of the Americas, New York, New York 10020

This Simon Spotlight edition August 2019

© 2019 Universal Studios and Shanghai Pearl Studio Film and Television Technology Co. All Rights Reserved.

All rights reserved, including the right of reproduction in whole or in part in any form.

SIMON SPOTLIGHT, READY-TO-READ, and colophon are registered trademarks of Simon & Schuster, Inc.

For information about special discounts for bulk purchases, please contact Simon & Schuster Special Sales at

1-866-506-1949 or business@simonandschuster.com.

Manufactured in the United States of America 0719 LAK

2 4 6 8 10 9 7 5 3 1

ISBN 978-1-5344-5066-0 (hc)

ISBN 978-1-5344-5065-3 (pbk)

ISBN 978-1-5344-5067-7 (eBook)

Hello! My name is Peng.
I am nine years old.

I love playing basketball.
One day I want to become
a basketball star!

I also love my best friend.
He is a yeti!
Do you want to meet him?

My best friend's name
is Everest.
His home is on a mountain.

His favorite food is pork buns.
He likes them more than I do . . .
and I really like pork buns!

I first met Everest
on the roof of my apartment.
He was hiding from
some bad guys.

My friend Yi, my cousin Jin, and I decided to take Everest back to his home.

We set off on our journey.
Soon I was thirsty,
so I drank a can of soda.

Everest had never tried
soda before.
He drank one can,
then a second can,
and then a third can.
After that, he didn't feel
very well!

After being thirsty,
I became hungry.
I daydreamed about dumplings
and pork buns.

Everest started humming,
and his fur glowed blue.
All of a sudden
giant blueberries started
to grow all around us!

The blueberries were delicious!
One of them exploded
all over Jin's clothes.
He was not happy.

The blueberries kept growing.
Soon they were bigger than
beach balls!

I also taught Everest
how to play thumb war.
He has really big thumbs.

He won the game, of course.

Later we found a field
of dandelion flowers.
I picked one
and closed my eyes.

I wished that I could be
a basketball star.
Then I blew on the seeds.

I picked another dandelion
for Everest.
"Make a wish," I said.

Everest thought
the dandelion looked
good enough to eat.
He ate it in one bite!

Then you'll never guess
what happened.
Everest started to hum,
and his fur glowed blue again.

Another dandelion grew and grew.
It was huge!

The dandelion lifted us into the air on a wild ride!

My best friend was
a magical yeti!

Our journey led us to a field
full of pretty yellow flowers.

This time Everest held back
from eating the flowers!

Everest was happy to have new friends, but he was also sad. He missed his family.

We needed to get him home quickly!

Finally we arrived at the mountain where Everest lived.

Once Everest was safely home,
it was time to say goodbye.

I gave Everest a big hug.
Even if we are far apart,
we will always be
best friends forever!